Frogs and Toads

Written by Jo Windsor

In this book you will see frogs and toads.

frog

toad

frogs

Frogs and toads can live on the land.

Frogs and toads can live in the water, too.

A frog can live...

in a bathtub Yes? No?

in a box Yes? No?

Look at the frog's skin!

It is wet.

A frog has to have wet skin.

frog

Look at the toad's skin!
It is bumpy.

toad

Look at the frogs!

Some frogs like to live in trees.

frogs

Look at the toad!

Toads can go up in trees, but they like to live on the ground.

toad

This frog is under the ground.

Some toads can go under the ground, too.

Frogs and toads can hide under the ground.

Why do frogs and toads hide under the ground?

frog

toad

Frogs and toads can jump!

Look at the frog's legs. Its legs help it jump.

This frog can jump from tree to tree!

Frogs and toads can...

jump	Yes? No?
fly	Yes? No?
swim	Yes? No?
hop	Yes? No?

Frogs and toads like to eat meat.

Frogs and toads can eat birds, mice, insects, and snakes!

frog

toad

frog

Look at the eggs!

The frog's eggs are in the water.

The toad's eggs are on its back.

Eggs can be...

in a nest   Yes? No?

in the water   Yes? No?

on a back   Yes? No?

frogs

toad

Look!

Tadpoles have come out of the eggs.

The tadpoles are on the frog's back.

tadpoles

The tadpoles stay in the water.
They get bigger.

The tadpoles grow legs.
Now they are frogs and toads.

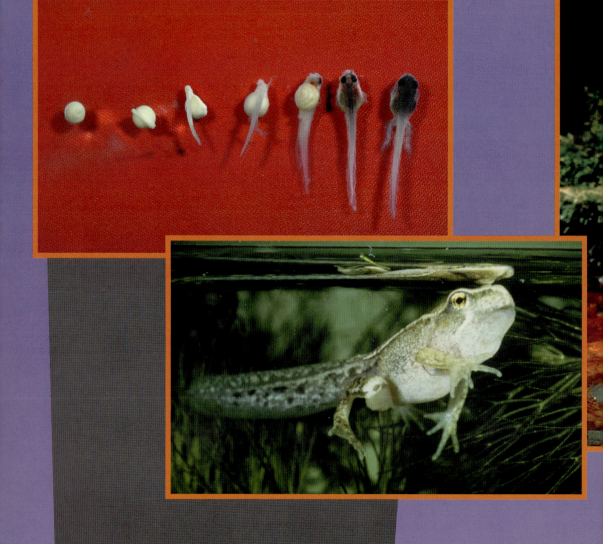

Index

eggs 16, 18

food 14

skin 6, 7

tadpoles . . .18, 19, 20

tree 8, 9

A yes/no chart

Frogs have dry skin. Yes? No?

Frogs eat meat. Yes? No?

frog

Toads have bumpy skin. Yes? No?

Toads can live in the water. Yes? No?

Frogs can hide under the ground. Yes? No?

toad

Toads can jump. Yes? No?

Toads live in trees. Yes? No?

Word Bank

eggs

tadpoles

insects

water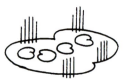

snake